Birthday Book Club

This book was donated
in honor of the birthday of

Bradley H. Lyle

by

Mom & Dad

January 13, 2007

ELVIS HORNBILL
INTERNATIONAL BUSINESS BIRD

BY STEVE SHEPARD

HENRY HOLT & CO. NEW YORK

One day soon after my wife, Jeanne, and I moved into our new house in Ouagadougou, a neighbor came into our yard carrying a box with a little bird in it. An orphaned hornbill had been found in the woods outside of town, and our neighbor wanted to know if we would give it a home.

THE INFANT HORNBILL

ARRIVES AT OUR HOUSE

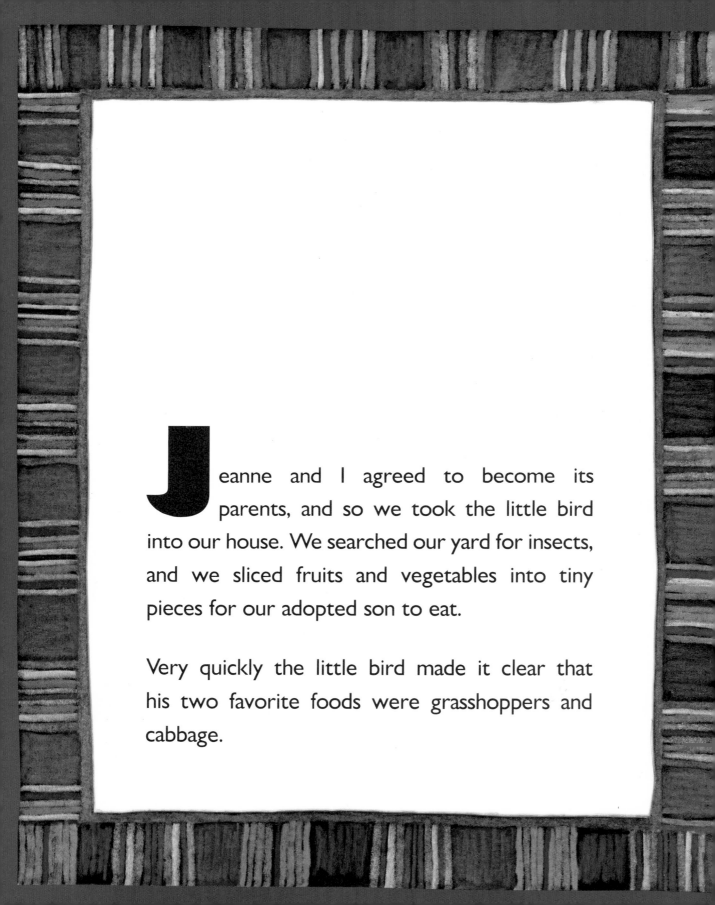

Jeanne and I agreed to become its parents, and so we took the little bird into our house. We searched our yard for insects, and we sliced fruits and vegetables into tiny pieces for our adopted son to eat.

Very quickly the little bird made it clear that his two favorite foods were grasshoppers and cabbage.

JEANNE AND I ADOPT

THE INFANT HORNBILL

OUR BABY BIRD

IS EAGER TO EAT

Our little bird had a good strong voice. He called loudly for his food, and expressed himself in songs throughout the day. I knew talent when I heard it. I wanted my son to become a singing star. I encouraged him to sing, and I named him "Elvis," after the great rock and roll star Elvis Presley.

OUR INFANT BIRD SINGS

HIS SINGING IS SO GOOD
WE NAME OUR SON "ELVIS"

At a very early age Elvis learned to read. He liked books about accounting and economics, and he read more and more of them as he got older. Instead of practicing his singing, he spent hours with a notepad and pencil, adding and subtracting figures.

YOUNG ELVIS STUDIES HARD

HIS FAVORITE SUBJECTS:
ACCOUNTING & ECONOMICS

I hoped Elvis's love of accounting was just a stage that he would grow out of. I played good rock and roll music all day long. I read fan magazines out loud, so Elvis could hear about the concerts rock and roll stars gave. I told him if he spent half the time playing guitar that he spent studying banking, he would be better than the King himself. I even encouraged him to let the feathers on his head grow out. But Elvis refused to play the guitar.

I hired a tailor to sew Elvis a sequined jacket like the one the King wore. I hoped Elvis would like it and change his mind about rock and roll. But he would not be caught dead in the shiny outfit. Then, after refusing to wear the sequined jacket, Elvis hired the tailor to make a business suit!

I was furious. How could he waste his talent for music? Why was he interested in something as frivolous as finance?

ELVIS GETS A BUSINESS SUIT

THE TAILOR MAKES A PERFECT FIT

J eanne told me not to force Elvis to study music. She said I should expose our son to the arts and let him make up his own mind about his career. I thought about this advice, and decided that Elvis should go to the annual art show held in Ouagadougou. Maybe seeing great paintings, baskets, and sculpture would get Elvis interested in the arts.

Elvis went, but he didn't care about the art exhibit. My son only cared about no-good useless business!

WE TAKE ELVIS TO SEE ART

ARTS AND CRAFTS

OUAGADOUGOU HAS A BIG
EXHIBITION EVERY YEAR

BASKETS & BRONZE STATUES

BEAK IN HIS MATH BOOK

Elvis began to keep track of the money Jeanne and I took to the market each week. He examined our groceries and counted the leftover change from our transactions. He was not satisfied with our purchases, so one day he decided to go shopping with us.

Elvis drove a hard bargain and managed to find better food at much better prices than we had been paying. He saved enough money to start a retirement fund for us.

ELVIS TAKES US SHOPPING

HE WANTS TO HELP US
BUY OUR FOOD AND GOODS

ELVIS BARTERS

HE MAKES SURE WE

FOR OUR FOOD

DON'T PAY TOO MUCH

In the month of April, when Elvis was nearly grown, Jeanne and I had to figure out how much money we owed the United States government. It was a difficult problem. We worked on it for hours, but we were stumped. Finally Elvis took the tax guide booklet and the tax tables from us, and Jeanne and I went to bed.

The next morning I found Elvis asleep on top of the finished tax returns. I knew talent when I saw it. I realized I had been wrong to want Elvis to sing. No matter what I thought of accounting, banking, or high finance, I must support my son in his pursuit of a business career.

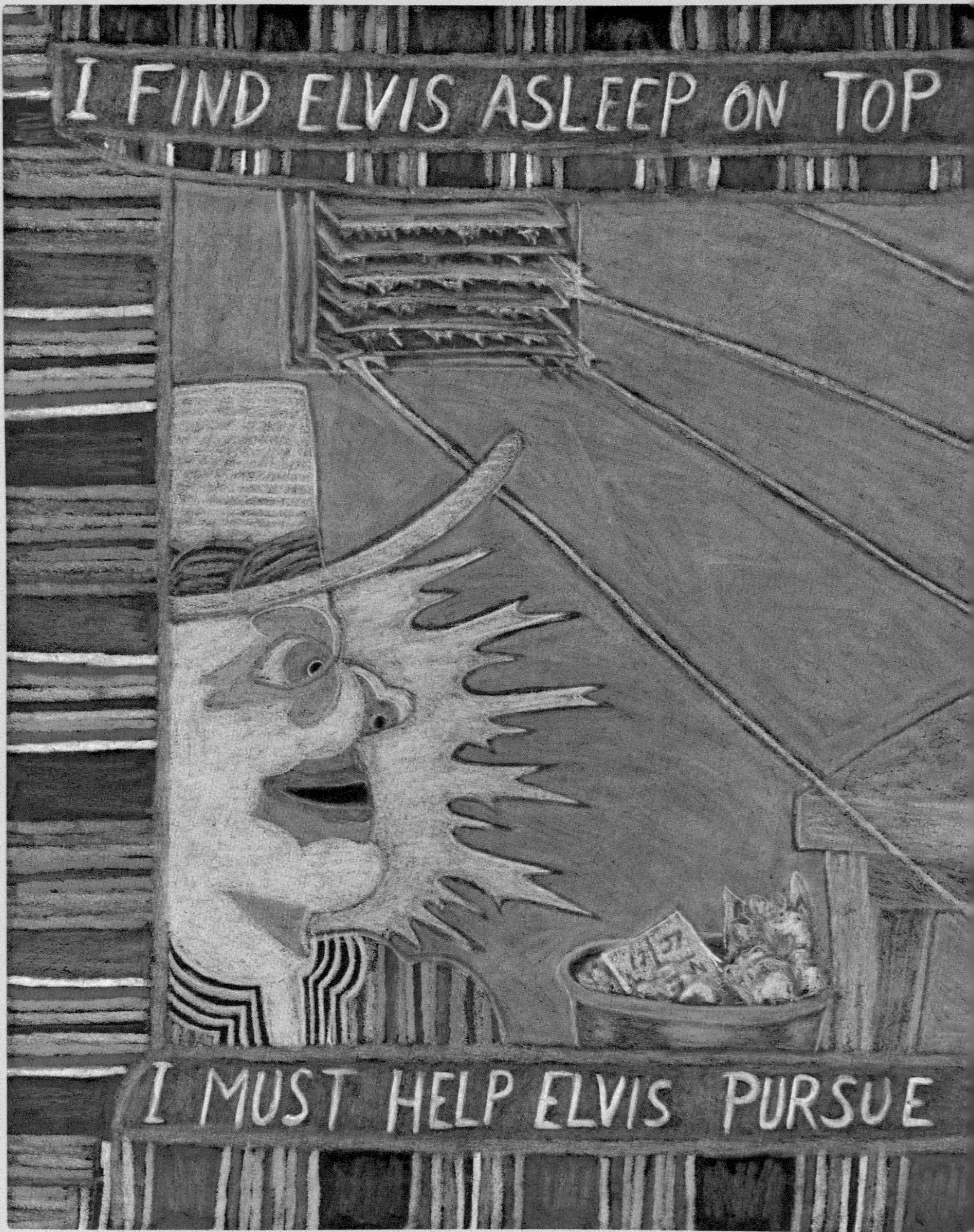
I FIND ELVIS ASLEEP ON TOP
I MUST HELP ELVIS PURSUE

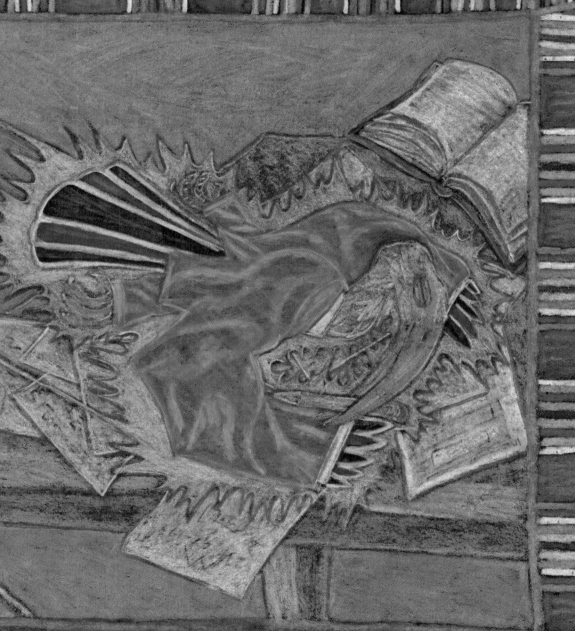

A BUSINESS CAREER

Soon the day arrived when Elvis felt ready to go to work in the field of international business. Jeanne and I put his resume and calculator into his briefcase, and he flew off for an interview at Ricardo's Hotel International. An hour later Elvis returned home with the news that he had been offered the job he wanted. He was the financial manager of Ricardo's.

Jeanne and I jumped for joy. We knew that our son would be happy in the life he had chosen. Elvis was not a rock and roll bird; he was an international business bird.

Dedicated to my wife, Jeanne Lebow,
and to my good friends Sawadago Salam
and Paulina Neira Julia

Copyright © 1991 by Steve Shepard
All rights reserved, including the right to reproduce
this book or portions thereof in any form.
First edition
Published by Henry Holt and Company, Inc.,
115 West 18th Street, New York, New York 10011.
Published simultaneously in Canada
by Fitzhenry & Whiteside Ltd.,
195 Allstate Parkway, Markham, Ontario L3R 4T8.

Library of Congress Cataloging-in-Publication Data
Shepard, Steve.
    Elvis Hornbill, international business bird / Steve Shepard.
    Summary: A father pushes his adopted son, a hornbill,
toward a musical career, even though the bird's interest and talent
lie in the field of finance.
    ISBN 0-8050-1617-1 (alk. paper)
    [1. Occupations—Fiction.   2. Hornbills—Fiction.   3. Fathers and
sons—Fiction.   4. Burkina Faso—Fiction.]   I. Title.
PZ7.S54325El   1991
[E]—dc20   90-44052

Henry Holt books are available at special discounts
for bulk purchases for sales promotions, premiums,
fund-raising, or educational use. Special editions
or book excerpts can also be created to specification.

Printed in the United States of America
on acid-free paper. ∞

10   9   8   7   6   5   4   3   2   1